We Shall Overcome

The Story of a Song

Written by Debbie Levy • Illustrated by Vanessa Brantley-Newton

Disney • JUMP AT THE SUN BOOKS

New York

In honor of the voices upon voices
who are the song's story

—D.L.

To the families and community of
Newtown, Connecticut

—V.B.N.

We shall overcome,
We shall overcome,

Text copyright © 2013 by Debbie Levy
Illustrations copyright © 2013 by Vanessa Brantley-Newton

First Edition
1 3 5 7 9 10 8 6 4 2
H106-9333-5-13244
The art was created in digital and mixed media.
Designed by Tyler Nevins
Printed in Malaysia
Library of Congress Cataloging-in-Publication Data is available.
ISBN 978-1-4231-1954-8
Reinforced binding
Visit www.disneyhyperionbooks.com

We shall overcome some day.

I am grateful to Thomas G. Hentoff for his thoughtful counsel and assistance in connection with this book.

—D.L.

We shall overcome,
We shall overcome,
We shall overcome some day.
Oh, deep in my heart
I do believe
We shall overcome some day.

We are not afraid,
We are not afraid,
We are not afraid today. . . .
We'll walk hand in hand,
We'll walk hand in hand,
We'll walk hand in hand some day. . . .

Information about other lyrics quoted in this book is found in "Sources," page 32.

I'll be all right,
I'll be all right,
I'll be all right some day.

Back in slavery times—
when enslaved people worked long days
with no pay and no say,
no freedom, no fairness,
no choice and no chance—
the people sang.

They suffered, yet they sang—
to soothe the hurt,
to fight the cruelty,
to declare that—yes!—they were human beings.

Oh, deep in my heart
I do believe
I'll be all right some day.

I'll overcome some day,

I'll overcome some day,

If in my heart I do not yield, I'll overcome some day.

It took a war—the Civil War—to end slavery.
But even after,
white people treated black people
as less than fully human,
excluding them, ignoring them,
blaming them,
even attacking them,
all because of the color of their skin.

Black people were no longer slaves,
it was true.
But they were not truly free.

Still they believed things would get better.
Still they sang.

We will overcome,
We will overcome,
We will overcome some day.

It wasn't easy to believe.
It wasn't easy when white people shut out African Americans from
good jobs and good pay,
schools and libraries and neighborhoods,
restaurants and hotels and bathrooms,
train cars and bus seats,
playgrounds and parks.
But black Americans, and some white Americans,
did believe they could overcome
the unfairness, hate, and violence.

They started to protest.
They brought a church song, "I Will Overcome,"
to the streets.
But since they were marching and working together,
they sang "*We* Will Overcome."
We, together, will overcome.

Oh, deep in my heart
I do believe
We will overcome some day.

We will organize

We will win our rights

We will win this fight

The union will see us through

Factory workers' protest, 1945-46

From the streets, the song reached the ears
of city people, country people,
followers and leaders.
It reached Martin Luther King,
the most important leader
working for justice for African Americans.
He took the song with him in his heart
everywhere he traveled.
The words changed a little.
But the spirit stayed the same.

We shall overcome,
We shall overcome,
We shall overcome some day.

Oh, deep in my heart
I do believe
We shall overcome some day.

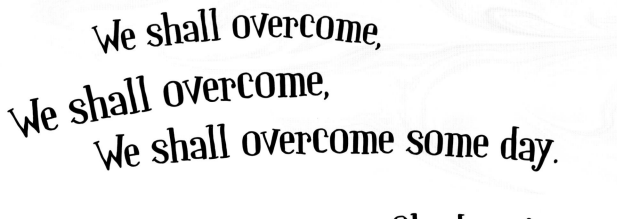

11

There were many forms of race hatred,
and many ways to fight it.
Some students fought by sitting down in restaurants
and asking to be served.
They didn't ask for free food.
They didn't want special service.
They just wanted to buy a meal,
like any white person could.

The students sat and sat,
waiting
for hamburgers, doughnuts, and sodas
that never came.
The students sat and waited until they were arrested,
and as they were taken away to jail,
they sang.

We are not afraid,
    We are not afraid,
We are not afraid today....

More and more people decided
to stand up for rights for African Americans.
One small group, the Freedom Singers,
traveled fifty thousand miles in nine months,
to living rooms, concert halls,
elementary schools, jails, high schools, and rallies,
bringing "We Shall Overcome"
to people in forty states,
inspiring them to believe
that change was coming.

We are not alone,
We are not alone,
We are not alone today....

Freedom Singers' first tour, 1962-63

The biggest gathering of people
united in support of fairness for African Americans
took place in the nation's capital.
Marching toward the Lincoln Memorial,
hundreds of thousands of people—
black and white and young and old—
joined hands,
joined voices,
and sang.

We'll walk hand in hand,

We'll walk hand in hand,

We'll walk hand in hand some day....

March on Washington, 1963

17

Speech by President Johnson, 1965

Slowly, slowly, things were changing.
Laws were passed.
But race hatred stayed strong,
even stronger than laws.
So President Lyndon Johnson gave a speech.
His ancestors once held slaves in Texas and Georgia,
but President Johnson looked out at the millions of people
watching him on television,
spoke of equal rights, human rights,
and voting rights for African Americans,

and recited the words of the song.

"We must overcome the crippling legacy of bigotry and injustice. And we shall overcome."

How could such a song stay in one country?
It could not.
"We Shall Overcome" sailed across the oceans
to other countries where people faced injustice.

It traveled to South Africa,
where black Africans embraced it as their own freedom song
in their long struggle against an all-white government
that treated them as outcasts in their own land.

Black and white together,
Black and white together,
Black and white together some day. . . .

We will live in peace,
We will live in peace,
We will live in peace some day....

The song traveled to India,
East Germany,
South Korea,
Czechoslovakia,
Northern Ireland,
Bangladesh,
China,
the Middle East,
South America—
wherever people worked
for a better life.

Even as it spread across the globe,
the song never really left its American home.
It took a very long time,
but race hatred did grow weaker.
Freedom grew stronger.
President Lyndon Johnson was followed
by another president and another,
another and another and another
and another and another,

   and then . . .

the people of the United States—
black and white and young and old—

elected an African American man to be their president.

On that day, people sang the song
that so many voices had sung before
in pain and in protest.

On that day, they sang in happiness.

Oh, deep in my heart I do believe
We shall overcome some day.

President Obama elected, 2008

CHANGE

CHANGE

CHANGE

CHANGE

Today, people still struggle
against hatred,
and for freedom,
against poverty,
and for fairness,
against despair,
and for hope.

We still sing.
We sing to declare that—yes!—we are all are human beings,
deserving of respect,
sharing the same planet,
the same future,
together.

The Life of "We Shall Overcome"

No single day marks the birth of the song "We Shall Overcome." No single person is its author. No single performance was the "first." Rather, "We Shall Overcome" is the product of many voices singing similar songs over many years in many places. As the songs passed from one person to another, the words and melodies changed, but the message of hope and determination stayed the same. Here are some notable milestones in the life of this song.

1800s: African Americans, enslaved and free, sing spirituals, or religious songs, in their worship services, at work, and at home. One such song is "I'll Be All Right."

1865: Slavery in the United States comes to an end.

Early 1900s: Some African Americans in Southern churches sing a song they call "I Will Overcome." The words and music are different from Reverend Tindley's song.

1900: Charles Albert Tindley, the son of former slaves and well-known pastor of a large African American church in Philadelphia, Pennsylvania, writes "I'll Overcome Some Day." The song becomes popular in black churches around the country.

1957: At a party where Dr. Martin Luther King, Jr. is a guest of honor, Pete Seeger sings "We Shall Overcome" for him for the first time. Dr. King was an important leader of the civil rights movement—people working for equal rights for all citizens, no matter their skin color.

1940s: Workers protest poor pay and conditions at a white-owned tobacco factory in Charleston, South Carolina. The black women workers march and sing the song they know from church, "I Will Overcome." Instead of "*I* will overcome," they sing "*We* will overcome."

Some workers attend the Highlander Folk School in Tennessee, where they share the song "We Will Overcome." Highlander is a school for adults—blacks and whites—working for fairness for all workers.

Folk singer Pete Seeger learns "We Will Overcome" at the Highlander School. Seeger and Septima Clark, a teacher at Highlander, change "We *will* overcome" to "We *shall* overcome."

Early 1960s: Folk singer Guy Carawan shares "We Shall Overcome" with civil rights activists around the country, many of them students. Activists conduct "sit-ins" at restaurants that deny them service because they are black. They take "Freedom Rides" to challenge race discrimination on buses and in bus stations. During many of these events, the participants are harassed, beaten, and put in jail. Through their ordeals, they sing "We Shall Overcome." The song becomes the anthem of the civil rights movement.

1962: The Freedom Singers form. Their performances of "We Shall Overcome" and other songs spread the word about, and also raise money for, the civil rights movement.

1963: On August 28, people come to the nation's capital for the "March on Washington for Jobs and Freedom." The marchers—hundreds of thousands of people—sing "We Shall Overcome." When they gather at the Lincoln Memorial, Dr. Martin Luther King, Jr., gives his famous "I Have a Dream" speech.

1964: Congress and the president adopt the Civil Rights Act of 1964, which makes it illegal to discriminate against people based on the color of their skin, in public facilities (such as restaurants, hotels, and stores), schools, and workplaces.

1965: On March 7, five hundred people march from Selma toward Montgomery, Alabama, to protest the ways white officials in that state prevent black citizens from exercising their right to vote. Soon after the marchers set out, Alabama police attack them with clubs, whips, and tear gas. Many marchers are injured, and the day becomes known as "Bloody Sunday."

A week later, President Lyndon B. Johnson gives a speech: "We must overcome the crippling legacy of bigotry and injustice. *And we shall overcome.*" President Johnson's speech is followed by the passage of the Voting Rights Act of 1965, a strong law to guarantee African Americans the right to vote in elections.

1967: Young East Germans begin singing "We Shall Overcome" at meetings and rallies to protest the absence of freedom in their Communist country. More than twenty years later, a democratic government is established there.

1970s: "We Shall Overcome," adopted by black South Africans in the 1960s, continues to be their freedom song as they struggle against *apartheid*, the system of harsh antiblack laws and customs created by the all-white government. Decades later, the people of South Africa elect a government of black and white lawmakers, and apartheid is abandoned.

During the 1971 Bangladesh war for independence from Pakistan, the Calcutta (India) Youth Choir records a version of "We Shall Overcome," which becomes one of the best-selling Bengali language records ever.

1986: Thousands begin to demonstrate in cities in South Korea to protest their country's rule by military officials. The marchers sing "We Shall Overcome." The following year, South Korea begins its transition to a government of democratically elected leaders.

1989: People in Czechoslovakia sing "We Shall Overcome" in widespread protests that peacefully topple the Communist government, leading to the establishment of more democratic forms of government.

2001: On September 23, thirty thousand people gather in Yankee Stadium in New York City to remember the victims of the September 11 terrorist attacks. Led by the Harlem Boys and Girls Choir, they join hands and sing "We Shall Overcome."

2008: On November 4, Barack Obama is elected the first African American president of the United States. For many, the election and inauguration of the nation's first black president was an occasion to reflect on how much African Americans have overcome since the days of slavery—and to sing the anthem of the long struggle for equal rights, "We Shall Overcome."

Sources

Pages 4–5: "I'll be all right." Performed by blues singer Taj Mahal in *We Shall Overcome*, a documentary film by Jim Brown, Ginger Brown, Harold Leventhal, and George Stoney, 1989.

Pages 6–7: "I'll overcome some day." Rev. Charles Albert Tindley, in African American Heritage Hymnal, GIA Publications, 2001.

Pages 8–9: "We will overcome." *Broadsides: Songs and Ballads Sung by Pete Seeger.* Folkways Records FA 2456, 1964; and *Songs of Work and Protest*, by Edith Fowke and Joe Glazer (New York: Dover Publications 1973).

Pages 10–11: "We shall overcome." Musical and lyrical adaptation by Zilphia Horton, Frank Hamilton, Guy Carawan, and Pete Seeger. Inspired by African American Gospel Singing, members of the Food & Tobacco Workers Union, Charleston, South Carolina, and the southern Civil Rights Movement. TRO – © Copyright 1960 (renewed) and 1963 (renewed) Ludlow Music, Inc., New York, NY. International Copyright Secured. Made In U.S.A. All Rights Reserved Including Public Performance For Profit. Royalties derived from this composition are being contributed to the We Shall Overcome Fund and The Freedom Movement under the Trusteeship of the writers. Used by Permission.

Pages 12–13: "We are not afraid." Horton, Hamilton, Carawan, and Seeger; see above copyright information.

Pages 14–15: "We are not alone." *We Shall Overcome! Songs of the Southern Freedom Movement*, compiled by Guy and Candie Carawan for The Student Nonviolent Coordinating Committee (New York: Oak Publications 1963).

Pages 16–17: "We'll walk hand in hand." Horton, Hamilton, Carawan, and Seeger; see above copyright information.

Pages 18–19: President Johnson's speech. Lyndon Baines Johnson Library and Museum. http://www.lbjlib.utexas.edu/johnson/archives.hom/speeches.hom/650315.asp.

Pages 20–21: "Black and white together." *We Shall Overcome! Songs of the Southern Freedom Movement*; see above copyright information.

Pages 22–23: "We will live in peace." *Broadsides*; see above copyright information.

Pages 24–25: "Oh, deep in my heart." Horton, Hamilton, Carawan, and Seeger; see above copyright information.

You can listen to recordings of "We Shall Overcome" at these Web addresses on the Internet:

University of Virginia Library, *Lift Every Voice: Music in American Life, Protest Songs—We Shall Overcome.* http://www2.lib.virginia.edu/exhibits/music/protest_overcome.html. (The Freedom Singers, from *Voices of the Civil Rights Movement: Black American Freedom Songs, 1960–1966*, Smithsonian Folkways Recordings, 1997.)

National Public Radio, "A Freedom Singer Shares the Music of the Movement," February 11, 2010. http://www.npr.org/templates/story/story.php?storyId=123599617. (Singing led by civil rights activist Fannie Lou Hamer in Hattiesburg, Mississippi, 1964, from *Voices of the Civil Rights Movement* record.)

John F. Kennedy Center for the Performing Arts, ArtsEdge, "The Story Behind the Song: We Shall Overcome." http://artsedge.kennedy-center.org/students/features/story-behind-the-song/we-shall-overcome.aspx. (Contralto Marian Anderson; folk singer Joan Baez.)

Morehouse College Glee Club, "We Shall Overcome," April 3, 2009. http://www.youtube.com/watch?v=Aor6-DkzBJ0.

For Further Reading

Davis Pinkney, Andrea. *Sit-In: How Four Friends Stood Up by Sitting Down.* Illustrated by Brian Pinkney. New York: Little, Brown, 2010.

Evans, Shane W. *We March.* New York: Roaring Brook Press, 2012.

Levine, Ellen. *If You Lived at the Time of Martin Luther King.* Illustrated by Anna Rich. New York: Scholastic, 1994.

Ramsey, Calvin Alexander. *Ruth and the Green Book.* Illustrated by Floyd Cooper. Minneapolis: Carolrhoda, 2010.

Rappaport, Doreen. *Free At Last! Stories and Songs of Emancipation.* Illustrated by Shane W. Evans. Cambridge, Mass.: Candlewick Press, 2003.

Rappaport, Doreen. *Nobody Gonna Turn Me 'Round! Stories and Songs of the Civil Rights Movement.* Illustrated by Shane W. Evans. Cambridge, Mass.: Candlewick Press, 2005.

Shelton, Paula Young. *Child of the Civil Rights Movement.* Illustrated by Raul Colón. New York: Schwartz and Wade, 2009.

Stotts, Stuart. *We Shall Overcome: A Song that Changed the World.* Illustrated by Terrance Cummings. New York: Clarion, 2010.